Rikki-Tikki-Tavi

A story about a mongoose
by Rudyard Kipling

LEVEL  READER

Adapted by Kathryn Knight
Illustrated by Ruth Palmer

D0199361

This is the story of the great war that Rikki-tikki-tavi fought single-handed, through the bathrooms of the big house. Darzee the Tailorbird helped him. Chuchundra the Muskrat warned him. But Rikki-tikki did the real fighting.

He was a mongoose. He was like a little cat in his fur and his tail, but quite like a weasel in his head and his habits. His eyes and the end of his restless nose were pink. He could scratch himself anywhere he pleased with any leg, front or back. He could fluff up his tail till it looked like a brush. And his war cry, as he scuttled through the long grass, was *Rikk-tikk-tikki-tikki-tchk*!

One day, a high summer flood washed him out of the underground den where he lived with his father and mother. The flood carried him, kicking and clucking, down a roadside ditch. He found a little wisp of grass floating there, and he clung to it.

When the ground dried, there he lay all soggy in the hot sun on the middle of a garden path. A small boy was saying, "Here's a dead mongoose."

"Let's take him in and dry him," said his mother. "Perhaps he isn't really dead."

They took him into the house. A big man picked him up between his finger and thumb. He smiled and said, "Not dead. Just half drowned." So they wrapped him in cloth and warmed him over a little fire.
He opened his eyes and sneezed.

"Now," said the big man (he was an Englishman who had just moved to India), "don't frighten him, and we'll see what he'll do."

It is hard to frighten a mongoose. A mongoose is eaten up from nose to tail with curiosity, and Rikki-tikki was a true mongoose. He perked up, ran all round the table, sat up, scratched himself, and jumped on the small boy's shoulder.

"Don't be frightened, Teddy," said his father. "That's his way of making friends."

"Oh! He's tickling under my chin," said Teddy.

Rikki-tikki snuffed at the boy's ear. Then he climbed down to the floor and rubbed his nose.

"Oh, my," said Teddy's mother, "and he's a wild creature! I suppose he's so tame because we've been kind to him."

"All mongooses are like that," said her husband. "If Teddy doesn't pick him up by the tail, or try to put him in a cage, he'll run in and out of the house all day long. Let's give him something to eat."

They gave him a little piece of meat. Rikki-tikki liked it very much. After he ate, he went out onto the porch and sat in the sunshine and fluffed up his fur so it would dry. Then he felt better.

"There are many things to find out about in this house," he said to himself. "I will stay."

He spent all that day roaming over the house. He almost drowned in the bathtub. He climbed up into the big man's lap at the writing table. He even put his nose into the inkwell.

At nightfall he ran to Teddy's room to watch how lamps were lighted. When Teddy went to bed, Rikki-tikki climbed up too. Teddy's mother and father came in to say goodnight. There was Rikki-tikki awake on the pillow.

"I don't like that," said Teddy's mother. "He may bite the child."

"He'll do no such thing," said the father. "Teddy's safer with that little beast than with a watchdog. If a snake came into the room now—"

But Teddy's mother wouldn't think of anything so awful.

Early in the morning, Rikki-tikki came to breakfast riding on Teddy's shoulder. They gave him banana and boiled egg. He sat on all their laps one after the other. He enjoyed being a house-mongoose.

Then Rikki-tikki went out into the garden to see what was to be seen. It was a large garden with big bushes, lime and orange trees, and clumps of bamboo and high grass.

Rikki-tikki licked his lips. "This is a splendid hunting ground," he said. His tail grew brushy and he scuttled up and down the garden, snuffing.

He heard sad voices in a thorn bush. It was Darzee the Tailorbird and his wife. They had made a beautiful nest, but they sat there crying.

"What is the matter?" asked Rikki-tikki.

"One of our babies fell out of the nest yesterday," said Darzee, "and Nag ate him."

"Hm!" said Rikki-tikki. "That is very sad—but I am a stranger here. Who is Nag?"

Darzee and his wife hid in their nest and did not answer. From the thick grass there came a low hiss— a horrid cold sound that made Rikki-tikki jump back. Then inch by inch out of the grass rose up the head and wide hood of Nag, the big black cobra. He was five feet long from tongue to tail. He lifted himself and swayed back and forth, looking at Rikki-tikki with wicked eyes.

"Who is Nag?" said he. "*I* am Nag. Look, and be afraid!"

Rikki-tikki was afraid for a moment. But it is impossible for a mongoose to stay frightened for long. Rikki-tikki had never met a live cobra before, but his mother had fed him dead ones, and he knew it was a mongoose's job to fight and eat snakes. Nag knew that too—and *he* was afraid.

"Well," said Rikki-tikki, and his tail began to fluff up again, "do you think it is right for you to eat chicks from a nest?"

Nag was watching the grass behind Rikki-tikki. Nag knew that mongooses in the garden meant death sooner or later for him and his family. So he dropped his head a little and spoke quietly.

"Let us talk," he said. "*You* eat eggs. Why shouldn't *I* eat *birds*?"

"Behind you! Look behind you!" sang Darzee.

Rikki-tikki jumped high in the air just as something whizzed by under him. It was the head of Nagaina, Nag's wicked wife. She had crept up to make an end of him, but had missed. Rikki-tikki came down almost across her back. If he had been an old mongoose, he would have known to break her back with one hard bite. But he was afraid and he did not bite long enough. He jumped clear of her whisking tail.

"Wicked, wicked Darzee!" said Nag. The snake lashed up at the nest, but it was too high.

When a mongoose's eyes grow red, he is angry. Rikki-tikki's eyes were red! He sat back on his tail like a little kangaroo and looked all round him. But Nag and Nagaina had disappeared into the grass.

Rikki-tikki trotted off to the house and sat down to think. It was a serious matter for him. He was a young mongoose, and it pleased him to think that he had escaped a blow from behind. When Teddy came running down the path, Rikki-tikki was ready to be petted.

Just as Teddy was stooping, something wriggled a little in the dust. A tiny voice said:

"Be careful. I am Death!"

It was Karait, the small brown snake with a bite as dangerous as the cobra's.

Rikki-tikki's eyes grew red again. He danced up to Karait and swayed back and forth in the way mongooses do. It looks very funny, but it helps when avoiding the quick movements of a snake. Karait struck out. Rikki jumped sideways. The little snake's head lashed once more, and Rikki-tikki sprang over the wiggling body.

Teddy shouted, "Oh, look here! Our mongoose is killing a snake!" Teddy's mother screamed. His father ran out with a stick. Karait snapped, and Rikki-tikki jumped onto the snake's back. He bit the snake near its head, and the snake lay still.

Teddy's father began to beat the dead Karait.

What is the use of that? thought Rikki-tikki. *I have settled it all.*

And then Teddy's mother picked Rikki-tikki up and hugged him. Teddy's father said that he was sent from heaven. Teddy looked on with big scared eyes. Rikki-tikki was amused at all the fuss, which, of course, he did not understand.

That night at dinner, he walked all over the table, but he did not stuff himself. He wanted to stay ready to fight Nag and Nagaina. Sometimes he gave his long war cry: *Rikk-tikk-tikki-tikki-tchk!*

Teddy carried him off to bed and tucked him under his chin. But as soon as Teddy was asleep, Rikki-tikki went off for his nightly walk around the house. In the dark he met Chuchundra the Muskrat creeping around by the wall.

"Don't kill me," said Chuchundra quietly. "Rikki-tikki, don't kill me!"

"Do you think a snake-killer kills muskrats?" laughed Rikki-tikki.

"Hush! Nag is everywhere. Can't you *hear*, Rikki-tikki?"

Rikki-tikki listened.

Scratch-scratch-scratch-scratch.

"That's Nag or Nagaina," Rikki-tikki said, "crawling into a bathroom drain!"

He scurried to Teddy's bathroom. Nothing there. In the mother's bathroom, he put his little ear to the drain that led to the outside. He heard Nag and Nagaina whispering in the moonlight.

"When the people are gone," said Nagaina, "*he* will have to go away, and then the garden will be ours again. Go in quietly, husband. Bite the big man first. Then come out and tell me, and we will hunt for Rikki-tikki together."

"But are you sure we should kill the people?" said Nag.

"Ssss! With no people, there will be no more mongoose. As long as the house is empty, we are king and queen of the garden. And remember—when our eggs in the melon bed hatch tomorrow, our children will need room and quiet."

"I had not thought of that," said Nag. "I will go do the killings and return with no noise."

Rikki-tikki tingled with rage. He saw Nag's head come through the drain. His five feet of cold body followed it. Rikki-tikki was frightened. Nag coiled up, raised his head, and looked into the dark bathroom. Rikki could see his eyes glitter.

If I kill him here, thought Rikki-tikki, *Nagaina will know. And I do not want to fight him on the open floor. What am I to do?*

Rikki-tikki heard Nag drinking from a big water jar. "That is good," said the snake. "Now, when Karait was killed, the big man had a stick. When he comes in for his bath in the morning he will not have a stick. I will wait here till he comes. Nagaina—do you hear me?—I will wait here in the cool till daytime."

There was no answer. Nagaina had left. Nag coiled himself down at the bottom of the water jar. Rikki-tikki stayed still as death. After an hour he began to move, little by little, toward the jar. Nag was asleep. Rikki-tikki looked at his big back. *If I don't break his back at the first jump*, thought Rikki, *he can still fight. And if he fights—oh, Rikki!* A bite near the tail would only make Nag wild.

It must be the head. The head above the hood. And, when I am there, I must not let go.

Then he jumped. Nag's head was lying a little clear of the water jar—and Rikki's teeth bit down!

The snake sprang up and whipped his body, shaking the mongoose like a rat, up and down, and around in great circles. Rikki's eyes were red and he held on! *Clang!* The snake's tail hit the tin dipper and the soap dish—*crack!*—against the side of the bath.

Rikki closed his jaws tighter and tighter. He was sure he would be banged to death. He was dizzy. He felt shaken to pieces. Suddenly—*bang!*—something went off like thunder just behind him. A hot, red fire burned his fur. The big man had fired a shotgun into Nag.

Rikki-tikki held on with his eyes shut, for now he was quite sure he was dead. But the snake's head did not move. Rikki loosened his bite.

The big man picked Rikki up and called, "It's the mongoose again, Alice. The little chap has saved *our* lives now."

Teddy's mother came in with a very white face and saw what was left of Nag.

Then Rikki-tikki dragged himself to Teddy's bedroom and snuggled under the boy's chin.

In the morning, Rikki-tikki was very stiff but quite pleased with himself. "Now I have Nagaina to deal with," he said. "She will be worse than five Nags. And who knows when her eggs will hatch! Goodness! I must go and see Darzee."

Rikki-tikki ran to the thorn bush. Darzee was singing a song at the top of his voice. The news of Nag's death was all over the garden.

"*Rikk-tck!*" said Rikki. "Is this the time to sing?"

"Nag is dead—is dead—is dead!" sang Darzee. "The brave Rikki-tikki caught him by the head. The big man brought the bang-stick, and Nag fell in two pieces! He will never eat my babies again."

"All that's true—but where's Nagaina?" said Rikki-tikki, looking carefully around.

"Oh, let us sing about the great, the red-eyed Rikki-tikki!" sang Darzee.

"Stop singing, Darzee!" said Rikki. "Where is Nagaina?"

"She is away at the stables, crying for Nag. Ah! Great is Rikki-tikki with the white teeth!"

"Never mind my white teeth! Where does she keep her eggs?"

"In the melon bed, near the wall. She hid them there weeks ago. Rikki-tikki, surely you are not going to eat her eggs!"

"Not eat exactly, no. Darzee, fly off to the stables and pretend that your wing is broken. Let Nagaina chase you to this bush. I must get to the melon bed, and if I went there now she'd see me."

Darzee was a silly little fellow, but his wife had sense. She knew that cobra's eggs meant young cobras later on. So she flew off from the nest and left Darzee to keep the babies warm and sing his song about the death of Nag.

She fluttered in front of Nagaina and cried out, "Oh, my wing is broken!"

Nagaina lifted up her head and hissed.

"You! You are the one who warned Rikki-tikki when I would have killed him!" Nagaina moved toward the bird as it fluttered away.

Rikki-tikki heard them coming up the path. He raced for the melon patch near the wall. There he found twenty-five eggs hidden among the leaves and grass. He could see the baby cobras curled up inside the skin. He began to bite off the tops of the eggs as fast as he could.

"Rikki-tikki!" screamed Darzee's wife. "I led Nagaina toward the house. She has gone onto the porch! Oh, come quickly—she means to kill!"

Rikki-tikki raced from the melon bed, holding the last egg in his mouth. He scuttled up to the porch where Teddy and his mother and father were having breakfast. But they were not eating. They sat stone still, and their faces were white. Nagaina was coiled up next to Teddy's chair near his bare leg! She was swaying to and fro!

"Oh, foolish people who killed my Nag!" hissed Nagaina.

"Sit still, Teddy," whispered his father. "You mustn't move. Teddy, keep still."

Then Rikki-tikki came up and cried, "Look at your very last egg, Nagaina!"

The big snake spun around and saw the egg on the porch. "Ah-h! Give it to me," she said.

Rikki-tikki saw Teddy's father grab Teddy and drag him safely out of reach of Nagaina.

"Tricked! Tricked! *Rikk-tck-tck!*" chuckled Rikki. "The boy is safe, and it was I—I—I that caught Nag last night in the bathroom." He began to jump up and down. "I did it! *Rikki-tikki-tck-tck!* Come, Nagaina. Come and fight with me!"

Rikki-tikki's eyes were like hot coals. Nagaina flung out at him. Rikki-tikki jumped up and backward. Again and again and again she struck, and each time her head came with a whack on the porch. Then Rikki-tikki danced in a circle around her. Nagaina spun—and grabbed up the egg into her mouth. She flew like an arrow down the path, with Rikki-tikki behind her.

As he was running, Rikki-tikki heard Darzee still singing his foolish little song. But Darzee's wife was wiser. She flew down and flapped her wings about Nagaina's head and slowed her down. When the snake plunged into the hole where she and Nag used to live, Rikki's little white teeth were on her tail, and he went down with her. (Very few mongooses care to follow a cobra into its hole.)

Up in the nest, Darzee said sadly, "It is all over with Rikki-tikki! We must sing his death song. Valiant Rikki-tikki is dead! For Nagaina will surely kill him underground."

Just as Darzee began to sing a sad, sad song, a dusty, panting mongoose dragged himself out of the hole, licking his whiskers. Darzee stopped with a little shout. Rikki-tikki shook some of the dust out of his fur and sneezed. "It is all over," he said. "The snake will never come out again."

Rikki-tikki curled up in the grass and slept, for he had done a hard day's work. When he awoke, he said, "Now I will go back to the house. Darzee, tell everyone in the garden that Nagaina is dead."

The happy news set all the birds in the garden singing and the frogs croaking.

When Rikki got to the house, Teddy and Teddy's mother (she still looked very white) and Teddy's father came out and almost cried over him. That night they fed him all that he wished. And when Teddy's mother came in to say goodnight, here was Rikki curled under Teddy's chin.

"He saved our lives and Teddy's life," she said to her husband. "Just think—he saved all our lives."

Rikki-tikki woke up and chuckled, for he was proud of himself. But he did not grow too proud. He kept that garden as a mongoose should keep it, with tooth and jump and spring and bite, till never a cobra dared show its head inside the walls.

Darzee's Song

Who has delivered us, who?
    Tell me his nest and his name.
Rikki, the valiant, the true,
Tikki, with eyeballs of flame,
Rikk-tikki-tikki, the ivory-fanged,
    the hunter with eyeballs of flame!